OUTBACK
ADVENTURE

Frané Lessac and Mark Greenwood

Publishers

First published 1994
Reprinted 2000, 2002, 2004, 2006, 2009, 2015 by Artbeat Publishers
PO Box 1110 Fremantle, Western Australia 6160
Telephone: + 61 (08) 9430 5479 Facsimile: + 61 (08) 9431 7754
Email: artbeat@ozemail.com.au   www.artbeatpublishers.com

Typeset in Bookman
Colour separations by Pretone Graphics, Perth
ISBN 978-0-646-40600-8

Printed and bound in China by Everbest Printing Co. Ltd.

For Nana Goldie

An outback adventure began on this day,
south of Coolgardie, far, far away.
An aeroplane circled and gently touched down
on the desolate runway of an old ghost town.
It was Christmas time, nearly forty degrees,
and waiting for Cody in the shade of the trees
were Napuru, Nangala and old Uncle Max.
They'd driven all day over bumpy bush tracks.

Uncle Max brought his dog,
her name was Sheila.
Some say she was dingo,
some say blue heeler.
Studying a map they made a plan,
packed supplies and the
journey began.
They headed north on
a twisted track,
past six huge 'boomers'
to the great outback.

By a rugged gorge with high cliff walls,
they fished and swam near waterfalls.
When the billy boiled they stopped to eat
fresh barramundi as a lunchtime treat.
Uncle Max cooked damper on the open fire,
as the midday sun grew hotter and higher.

They panned for gold by a sandy stream.

Their rusted pans began to gleam.

Uncle Max held a nugget in disbelief,

"I think we've discovered Lasseter's Reef."

That night they settled
around their camp,
and sat by the light of a
kerosene lamp.
Uncle Max told a tale of how
one Christmas Day,
six white boomers towed
Santa's sleigh.
As the camp fire crackled,
they heard dingoes howl,
and a mopoke hoot
from a boobook owl.

Early next morning as thunder roared,
lightning flashed and summer rain poured.
Through puddles of mud with a shove and a push,
they drove past boabs back into the bush.

At the Bungle Bungles they looked to the top,
wedge-tailed eagles perched on a rock.
They saw race-horse goannas, blue-tongues too,
an eagle saw breakfast and down it flew.

Among the rocks in a shady place,
Napuru painted on Cody's face.
Nangala drew stories on gum tree bark,
with ochre and charcoal they made their mark.

With a wooden dish and
digging stick,
they collected food for a
bush picnic;
bush onions, bush currants,
sweet honey from bees
and ants from the base of
mulga trees.
They ate yams and sugar bread,
seeds and roots,
for dessert they feasted on
native fruits.

Nearby was a station where in the red dust
stockmen rode horses the colour of rust.
Cracking their whips they mustered the cattle,
the 'chopper' hovered with a hum and a rattle.

As thirsty crows cawed
and cicadas clicked,
the bushflies buzzed and horse
tails flicked.
The stockmen gathered for
a rodeo,
Uncle Max decided he'd
"ave a go".
He rode a bull they called
"True Blue".
It bucked and reared
through the air he flew!

They danced that night in the dust and sand,

to the music of a Country and Western band.

The group played fiddle, guitar and drums,

and a washboard strummed with thimbles on thumbs.

Later that evening it was time to leave.

What fun they'd had that Christmas Eve.

Cody lay in his swag and started to dream,

of his outback adventure and all he'd seen.

Suddenly he saw something dash through the sky,

he could not believe what he saw pass by.

Santa waved to Cody as he went on his way,

with six white boomers towing his sleigh.

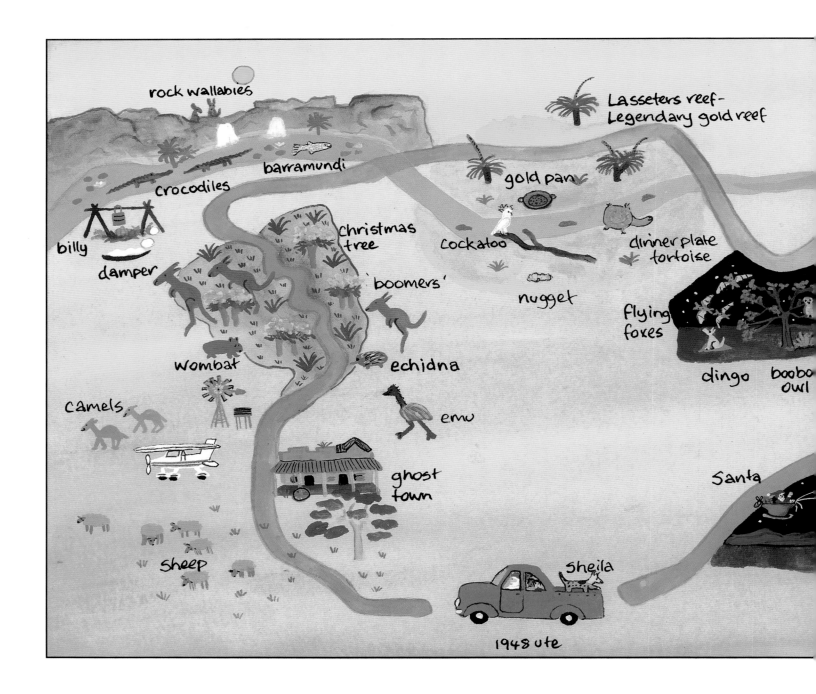

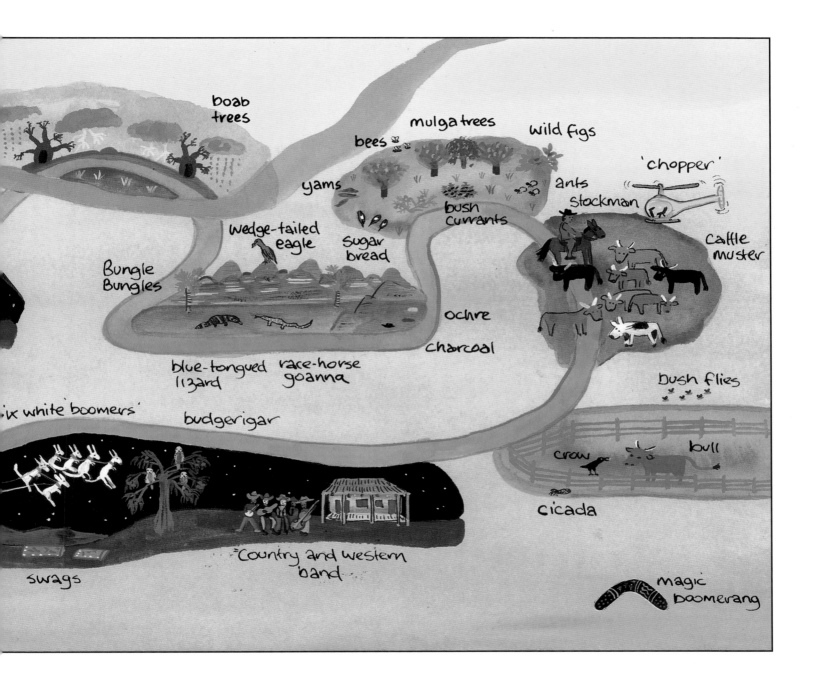

boab trees

mulga trees

bees

wild figs

'chopper'

yams

ants

stockman

bush currants

cattle muster

Wedge-tailed eagle

Sugar bread

Bungle Bungles

ochre

charcoal

bush flies

blue-tongued lizard

race-horse goanna

ix white boomers'

budgerigar

crow

bull

cicada

Country and western band

swags

magic boomerang

Frané Lessac has illustrated numerous popular children's books. Her books offer an insight into a range of cultures and have been translated into various languages. Frané's paintings have been exhibited in galleries throughout the world, including England, France, the United States, the Caribbean and Australia. After spending some years in the Caribbean she now lives in Fremantle with her family.

Mark Greenwood has contributed to two Caribbean titles illustrated by Frané Lessac. Outback Adventure is his third Australian book after the success of Magic Boomerang and Our Big Island. Mark is also a musician and has spent many years in the United States and England recording and performing. He is now based in Fremantle where he lives with his wife and two children.

Special thanks to:
Lynda and Bernie Ryder, Susan Dangen and Michelle MacGregor.

Frané & Mark